I'LL DO IT TOMORROW.
VROOM!
I FEEL FINE.
D0055938
FEARLESS FISH
GOOF-OFF GOOSE
HEALTHY HIPPO
IMITATING IGUANA
JEALOUS JACKAL
YES!
?
BUSY, BUSY, BUSY.
I KNOW EVERYTHING.
I'LL HOLD MY BREATH!
POSITIVE PIG
QUESTIONING QUAIL
RESPONSIBLE RABBIT
SMARTY STORK
TEMPER TANTRUM TURTLE
YAK, YAK, YAK, YAK.
HERE THEY ARE
SWEET PICKLES®
All twenty-six of them
in stories with giggles
and tickles and awful pickles
I DO IT MY WAY!
YAKETY YAK
ZANY ZEBRA

In the world of *Sweet Pickles,* each animal gets into a pickle because of an all too human personality trait.

This book is about Kidding Kangaroo who doesn't know when to stop joking.

Books in the Sweet Pickles Series:

WHO STOLE ALLIGATOR'S SHOE?
SCAREDY BEAR
FIXED BY CAMEL
NO KICKS FOR DOG
ELEPHANT EATS THE PROFITS
FISH AND FLIPS
GOOSE GOOFS OFF
HIPPO JOGS FOR HEALTH
ME TOO IGUANA
JACKAL WANTS MORE
WHO CAN TRUST YOU, KANGAROO?
LION IS DOWN IN THE DUMPS
MOODY MOOSE BUTTONS
NUTS TO NIGHTINGALE
OCTOPUS PROTESTS
PIG THINKS PINK
QUAIL CAN'T DECIDE
REST RABBIT REST
STORK SPILLS THE BEANS
TURTLE THROWS A TANTRUM
HAPPY BIRTHDAY UNICORN
KISS ME, I'M VULTURE
VERY WORRIED WALRUS
XERUS WON'T ALLOW IT!
YAKETY YAK YAK YAK
ZIP GOES ZEBRA

Library of Congress Cataloging in Publication Data

Hefter, Richard.
Who can trust you, kangaroo?
(Sweet Pickles series)
SUMMARY: Kangaroo discovers that his kidding and tricks do not always amuse his friends.
[1. Kangaroos–Fiction] I. Title. II. Series.
PZ7.H3587Wh [E] 78-16748
ISBN 0-03-042031-8

Published simultaneously in Canada by Holt, Rinehart and Winston of Canada, Limited.

Printed in the United States of America

Weekly Reader Books' Edition

Written and illustrated
by Richard Hefter
Edited by Ruth Lerner Perle

Holt, Rinehart and Winston • New York

Hippo was jogging around Kangaroo's house one morning. Suddenly he heard a cry from inside.

"Help!" the voice called. "I'm stuck in here."

Hippo rushed over. "Hold on!" he puffed. "I'll help you."

"Push the door open!" called the voice.

Hippo pushed and pushed. The door flew open with a crash and Hippo went tumbling in. SPLASH! A bucket of water dumped onto his head.

“Ugh! Wooph!” groaned Hippo. “I’m all wet. What happened?”

“Haw, haw!” laughed Kangaroo. “It was just a joke and you fell for it!”

“What about your call for help?” asked Hippo. “Weren’t you in trouble?”

"Nope," giggled Kangaroo. "I was only kidding! I just wanted to have some fun."

"That's not a very nice thing to do," grumbled Hippo. "You should never call for help unless you really need it."

"Haw, haw! I was only kidding," laughed Kangaroo.

"And it's not nice to dump water on people either!" shouted Hippo, as he jogged off in his wet sneakers. SPLISH, SPLOSH, SPLISH, SPLOSH.

Fish was riding her motorcycle past the park when she heard a shout.

"Help!" cried a voice. "Help me! Hurry! Help!"

Fish gunned her engine. VROOOOM! She swerved onto the grass.

“HELLLLP!” screeched the voice from behind the bushes.

“Don’t worry!” shouted Fish. “It’s Fearless Fish to the rescue!” Fish zoomed around the tree, shot past the bench and flew over the bushes. VROOOOM! She landed right in the pond. SPLOOOSH!

Kangaroo sat on the edge of the pond holding his sides and laughing and giggling.

"Looks like *you* need help, Fish!" he laughed. "Haw, haw!"

"Was that you calling for help?" screamed Fish.

"YUP!" laughed Kangaroo. "But I was only kidding."

"That's not a nice thing to do!" yelled Fish. "You ought to be ashamed of yourself."

Fish dragged her motorcycle out of the pond and sputtered off. VROOOOM.

"It may not be nice," snickered Kangaroo, "but it sure was funny!"

Kangaroo left the park and started to walk down Fifth Street. "Wonder what I can do next?" he thought. "It sure is a quiet day."

He turned the corner and walked past Hippo's house.

Rabbit was next door working in his garden.

Kangaroo heard Rabbit humming to himself as he worked.

"Oh, boy!" he grinned. "I've got a great joke to pull on Rabbit!"

Kangaroo snuck around the garage very quietly and started to pull in the garden hose.

Rabbit was busy hoeing and mowing when, suddenly, he heard a shout.

"HELP!" cried a voice. "HELP ME!"

Rabbit dropped his hoe and rushed over to the garage. The voice seemed to be coming from inside. Rabbit pulled the door up.

SPLAAAAAASSHHHH! Water rushed out of the hose with a WHOOSH! It knocked Rabbit over and soaked him completely.

"Oh!" he moaned. "Oh, my. What happened?"

Kangaroo was in the garage sitting on Rabbit's workbench, and aiming the hose. He was laughing and laughing. Tears ran out of his eyes.

"Haw! Haw! Hoo! Hah!" he laughed. "You're the funniest thing I've seen all day! Haw! Haw!"

"I think that is rude and dangerous!" yelled Rabbit. "And I must ask you to leave my garage this minute!"

"I was only kidding," laughed Kangaroo as he trotted off.

Kangaroo was passing the Car Wash when he had another idea. "I know," he grinned. "There's time for one more great joke before supper. And I know just what it is."

He looked into the Car Wash. It was closed for the day. Kangaroo pushed the door open and peered inside. It was dark and empty. He went in.

"This will be great," he giggled. "I'll just sit here in the dark with my hand on the water switch! I can see it now. I hear folks walk by. I scream for help. They rush in. I hit the switch. And BLAM! They get ALL WET! HAW, HAW!"

Kangaroo sat and waited.

Rabbit and Hippo were talking outside Hippo's house when Fish drove by.

"We have to do something about Kangaroo," said Rabbit. "I'm awfully tired of getting soaked."

"Me, too," huffed Hippo.

"He even got *me* today," yelled Fish. "He's a menace!"

“It’s not only that,” said Rabbit. “The things he’s doing can be dangerous!”

“Let’s see if we can get him to stop,” said Hippo.

They started off down the street towards Kangaroo's house. They turned down Fourth Street and walked past the Car Wash. They heard a screech from inside.

"HHHELLLLLLPPPP!" screamed the voice.

"HELP MEEEE!"

"Hmm," said Rabbit. "That voice sounds familiar!"

"I'll check," said Fish. She climbed up on a box and peered into the window. "It's Kangaroo, all right," she said. "He's in there with his hand on the water switch."

"HHHELLLLLPPPP!" screeched the voice again.

Hippo smiled. "I have an idea," he whispered. "Come on!"

Rabbit and Fish followed Hippo around the Car Wash and quietly locked the back door. They locked the front door. Then they locked all the windows and waited. Kangaroo kept on shouting for help.

Pretty soon, Kangaroo got tired of shouting. "I was sure I heard someone out there," he mumbled. "Well, this is no fun. I think I'll go home."

Kangaroo went to the front door. He tried to open it. It was locked. "That's funny," he thought. He ran to the back door. He tried it. It was locked. "Hey!" he shouted. "What's going on?"

He ran to all the windows. They were locked.
Kangaroo started to pound on the doors with his fists.
"HEY!" he screamed. "HELP! IN HERE!
I'M STUCK IN HERE! HELP ME!"

Kangaroo cried and wailed and shouted and banged on the door. “HELLLLPPPP!” he screeched, “HELP MEEEE!”
He wailed and yelled and kicked and pounded until his voice was hoarse.

Then he started to cry. "I'm stuck in here," he sobbed, "I'll be stuck in here all night! This isn't very funny!"

Suddenly he heard a voice at the window. The voice said, "No, it isn't funny, is it, Kangaroo, when the joke's on you!"

"OK. OK," said Kangaroo. "Let me out!"

Rabbit, Hippo and Fish unlocked the door and let Kangaroo out of the Car Wash.

"Now you know how we feel when *you* play tricks on *us*!" they said. "I hope we can trust you from now on."

"Sure you can!" smiled Kangaroo. "That was a pretty good trick."

"I'll have to try it out on someone else soon.
Haw, haw!"

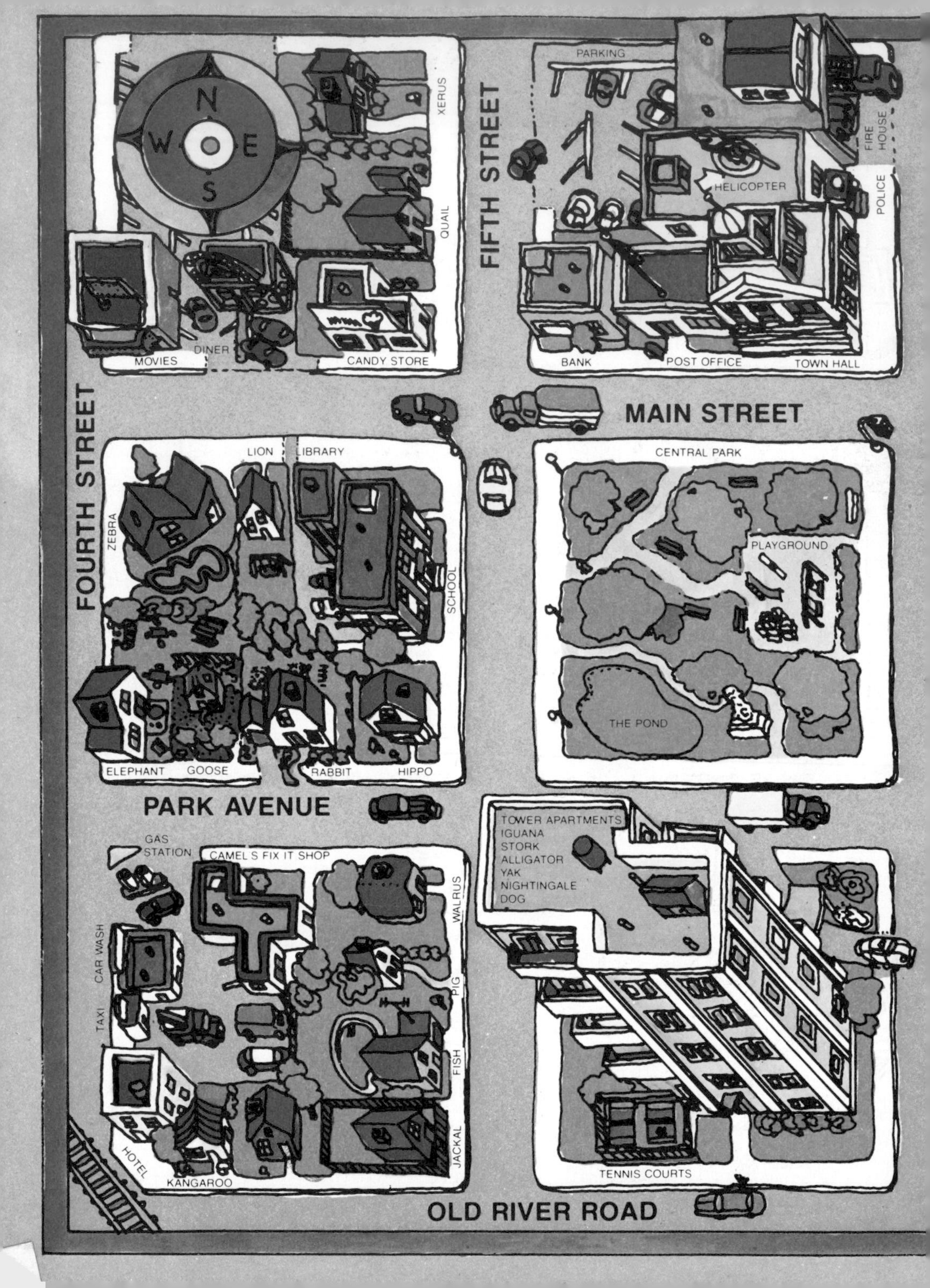
N
W
E
S
XERUS
QUAIL
MOVIES
DINER
CANDY STORE
PARKING
FIFTH STREET
FIRE HOUSE
HELICOPTER
POLICE
BANK
POST OFFICE
TOWN HALL
MAIN STREET
FOURTH STREET
LION
LIBRARY
ZEBRA
SCHOOL
ELEPHANT
GOOSE
RABBIT
HIPPO
CENTRAL PARK
PLAYGROUND
THE POND
PARK AVENUE
GAS STATION
CAMEL'S FIX IT SHOP
WALRUS
CAR WASH
TAXI
PIG
FISH
JACKAL
HOTEL
KANGAROO
TOWER APARTMENTS
IGUANA
STORK
ALLIGATOR
YAK
NIGHTINGALE
DOG
TENNIS COURTS
OLD RIVER ROAD